The History of Conservation
Preserving Our Planet

From Kyoto to Paris
Global Climate Accords

Jordan Johnson

Cavendish
Square
New York

Published in 2018 by Cavendish Square Publishing, LLC
243 5th Avenue, Suite 136, New York, NY 10016

Library of Congress Cataloging-in-Publication Data

Names: Johnson, Jordan, author.
Title: From Kyoto to Paris: global climate accords / Jordan Johnson.
Description: New York : Cavendish Square Publishing, 2018. | Series: The history of conservation: preserving our planet | Includes glossary, bibliography, and index. | Audience: Grades 9-12.
Identifiers: ISBN 9781502631244 (library bound) | ISBN 9781502631251 (ebook)
Subjects: LCSH: Climatic changes--Juvenile literature. | Climate change mitigation--Juvenile literature. | Global warming--Juvenile literature.
Classification: LCC QC903.15 J64 2018 | DDC 577.2'2--dc23

Editorial Director: David McNamara
Editor: Kristen Susienka
Copy Editor: Rebecca Rohan
Associate Art Director: Amy Greenan
Designer: Lindsey Auten
Production Coordinator: Karol Szymczuk
Photo Research: J8 Media

Printed in the United States of America

TABLE OF CONTENTS

Introduction

On December 24, 1968, a few photographs changed the world. Near the end of the **space race**, the astronauts aboard the Apollo 8 mission to the moon shared with people back on Earth a special broadcast of photographs of Earth and the surface of the moon. These were taken aboard the spacecraft, and a radio greeting from the astronauts could be heard by anyone listening in with a radio at home.

Earthrise and Its Impact

One of the most iconic photographs, *Earthrise*, captured the planet as a small and distant blue orb against a sea of the darkness of space. It publicly showed the world that there were no borders like those drawn on classroom maps. Earth was one entity. All earthlings had to share this space for the foreseeable future.

The experience of seeing all of Earth appearing so tiny and vulnerable deeply affected the astronauts. Astronaut Jim Lovell commented that "the vast loneliness is awe-inspiring, and it makes you realize just what you have back there on Earth."

Not long after Earth got the chance to view its first self-portrait from nearly 240,000 miles (386,242 kilometers) away, perspectives on the planet's health began to change. With the

Opposite: This photo, called *Earthrise*, became one of the most iconic images of Earth.

help of previous satellites launched during the United States' rivalry with the Soviet Union in the field of space exploration, the increasing movement toward environmental care began to gain momentum. In a few short years, a massive movement devoted to protecting our lonely blue marble began to grow more rapidly. It was clear that if the image of *Earthrise* was to be honored, it would require international cooperation the likes of which had not been seen before. For a world overshadowed by the Cold War, this was no simple task.

In 1990, at the suggestion of scientist Carl Sagan, the *Voyager 1* spacecraft took a picture of Earth from even farther away, showing it as a singular, pale blue dot from over 4 billion miles (6.4 billion km) away. The picture prompted Sagan to write in his book *Pale Blue Dot*: "Look again at that dot. That's here. That's home. That's us. On it everyone you love, everyone you know, everyone you ever heard of, every human being who ever was, lived out their lives … on a mote of dust suspended in a sunbeam."

As Sagan and other scientists have recognized and eloquently stated in the past, Earth is "the only home we've ever known." It is up to us to protect it. Over the past few decades, certain technologies have made humans more powerful and resilient than ever before. However, fuels and energies used to create these innovations are now causing a change in Earth's climate. This change may pose the greatest risk to the human race. If human beings are to preserve the planet and themselves, they need to recognize that this world is all we have. This can and has prompted nations to cooperate and take action. For instance, some countries have banded together to limit the emissions of **greenhouse gases** and the rise in global temperature.

The symbol of three green arrows folding over and leading to each other is the icon for recycling.

A United Effort

In the 1990s and 2010s, two significant agreements were made regarding these issues. They were the Kyoto Protocol and the Paris Agreement. Both treaties sought to bring nations together to fight the global threat of climate change in various ways. They took a bit of convincing and faced many obstacles, but both enlisted powerful nations and ultimately spoke to individuals. The messages they presented were clear: without action on our part, the planet as we know it will face a difficult and irreversible road of danger.

The Kyoto Protocol was created in the early 1990s. Just a few years before, world leaders had banded together to save Earth's **ozone layer**. The success of that effort gave the world hope that similar methods could be used. Many countries agreed that something needed to be done to protect the planet, and the Kyoto Protocol seemed to be the answer. The goal of the agreement was for countries involved to reduce the use of **fossil fuels**, which release carbon dioxide (CO_2) when burned. Carbon dioxide in the atmosphere is the leading cause of climate change. By reducing fossil fuel use, greenhouse gas emissions could be slowed or halted, and Earth's climate could be spared disastrous consequences.

However, the Kyoto Protocol proved ineffective. Many of the world's leading producers of greenhouse gases were either exempt or didn't commit to it. To make matters worse, some of the participating nations, like Canada, felt that the goals set by the protocol were unrealistic or impossible to achieve in the time provided. The architects of the Kyoto Protocol tried to fix these problems, but the damage was done. Many of the countries that previously were on board dropped out of the treaty. It was clear that a new arrangement needed to be made.

In 2015, the world got that new arrangement in the form of the Paris Agreement. It was bigger, broader, and had more achievable goals. It had goals for everyone to contribute to, and goals for specific nations. It was well received by more nations than the Kyoto Protocol. Some of the nations that weren't part of the last treaty were willing to participate in this new one. However, the Paris Agreement stands in jeopardy of failing like the Kyoto Protocol. Some people in positions of power have promised that their countries will not take part in the agreement. Other groups claim that the agreement's goals are not strict enough to make a difference. Just a few years after the agreement was passed, it seems that it too may prove ineffective.

Today, the future of the world in which we live is in danger. The international community is working to fix the problem, but so much stands in the way. The goals of global pacts cannot be too strict or too loose. The commitments must be realistic and binding.

While members of the **United Nations** and other international organizations work to preserve the earth, it is important to understand the history of previous international environmental agreements to help save the planet.

1

The Road to Kyoto

The Kyoto Protocol was an important step forward in a long journey of efforts to protect Earth. It was created in 1997 and had some very serious goals. It set out to get multiple nations to work together to protect the planet. It was necessary because scientists had observed that Earth's climate was changing, and human activity was largely to blame. More than one hundred years of burning fossil fuels had caused a change in Earth's atmosphere and its climate. If left unchecked, Earth's climate could change in ways that could make life for humans very difficult. Crops and other resources that require specific climates for growing could be harmed, for example.

Even before the issue of climate change took center stage, people were beginning to understand the effect humans had on the environment. For example, in 1963, the United States passed the Clean Air Act, a law meant to reduce air pollution

Opposite: Smokestacks, pictured here, are often associated with the large amounts of air pollution they can emit.

These soldiers from World War I are being taught how to quickly put on gas masks, devices that filter out dangerous substances from the air.

from factories and other industrial activity. In 1970, the National Environmental Policy Act made estimates on the environmental impact of federal projects a requirement. In the 1980s, a hole in Earth's ozone layer gained global attention.

The relationship between humans and nature has a long history, and in order to understand what led to the Kyoto Protocol, understanding that history is key.

The Industrial Age

A few hundred years ago, human society was very different. Back then, **agriculture** was a main way of life. Likewise, huge advancements in technology had not yet been made. Most people spent their time growing and maintaining their food supply. However, that changed during the Renaissance and the Age of Enlightenment, when artists and philosophers began challenging common ideas and exploring new technologies.

The 1700s and 1800s saw many new inventions and advances in technology, particularly for machines used in city factories and on farms. For this reason, the era from 1760 to 1900 was called the Industrial Revolution. One of the most important inventions for the era was the steam engine. Steam engines use the pressure created by boiling water to move machinery. Appearing in the late 1600s, before the Industrial Revolution began, the steam engine allowed large ships to travel across bodies of water and was used in machines to help farmers complete their work in half the time. In the 1800s, it was the main engine that allowed railcars to take supplies and people across countries. It was easy to see that steam-powered machines could make more items faster and with less effort than human power. However, there was a down side. Steam power depended on coal to function.

Coal is a fossil fuel created in Earth's crust. It is formed over millions of years, the result of tons of pressure being placed on the remains of ancient plants and animals. Because it was cheap and easy to find, coal was the main source of fuel and heat during the Industrial Revolution and for a long time after.

Burning coal, or any other fossil fuel, releases carbon dioxide. In small amounts, carbon dioxide is pretty harmless. Whenever someone exhales, they expel carbon dioxide naturally. Carbon dioxide even plays an important role in Earth's **ecosystem**. Plants absorb it and release oxygen, which humans and other animals need to breathe. However, after hundreds of years of burning fossil fuels, the amount of carbon dioxide in Earth's atmosphere has drastically increased. This is a problem because large quantities of carbon dioxide (and other gases, like methane and nitrous oxide) trap heat from the sun in Earth's atmosphere. This trapping of heat is called the **greenhouse effect**. It's called that because it resembles the effect of an actual greenhouse's ability to physically trap heat for the plants inside. Gases that cause the greenhouse effect are called greenhouse gases (GHGs).

As more and more factories arose throughout the Industrial Revolution, more carbon dioxide escaped into the atmosphere, gradually affecting the temperature on Earth. Some scientists, such as Svante Arrhenius and John Tyndall, predicted very early on that large amounts of carbon dioxide in the air might have lasting effects on the planet. However, to the average citizen, coal smoke and the carbon dioxide it emitted were seen as mostly annoyances. In the 1800s, various laws aiming to reduce coal smoke were passed in the United States and Europe, but they had little effect. Coal remained the main fuel source for people and businesses for more than one hundred years.

Greenhouse Gas Emissions from the Top Ten Producers of GHGs in 2011

2011 Total Emissions Country Rank	Country	2011 Total Carbon Dioxide Emissions from the Consumption of Energy (Million Metric Tons)	2011 Per Capita Carbon Dioxide Emissions from the Consumption of Energy (Metric Tons of Carbon Dioxide per Person)
1.	China	8,715.31	6.52
2.	United States	5,490.63	17.62
3.	Russia	1,788.14	12.55
4.	India	1,725.76	1.45
5.	Japan	1,180.62	9.26
6.	Germany	748.49	9.19
7.	Iran	624.86	8.02
8.	South Korea	610.95	12.53
9.	Canada	552.56	16.24
10.	Saudi Arabia	513.53	19.65

As time went on, coal became scarcer. People had to work harder and dig deeper to mine enough coal to keep up with the demand.

The beginning of the end of coal's time as the number one fuel source came in 1902. Coal miners in Pennsylvania went on strike, refusing to work. They went on strike because the work was dangerous, the pay was too little, and their shifts were too long.

fact!

One of the other big issues with coal was its contribution to dangerous environmental effects like "killer fogs." A series of poisonous fogs caused by coal pollution and natural environmental patterns killed thousands of people in London in the 1800s. Another deadly pollution-related fog occurred in London in 1952.

While the strike eventually ended, the coal shortages it created started to get people looking into other sources of fuel. This included crude oil (also known as petroleum oil or simply oil), natural gas, nuclear power, and renewable sources of energy like hydroelectric dams and wind turbines.

As cars became more popular in the 1920s and onward, gasoline made from oil became the main way to power them. Although not primarily used to generate electricity, oil is still one of the most dominant fuel sources today. Oil-based fuels are used to run cars, planes, and other vehicles that deliver people and goods all over the world.

Progressing in the 1980s and 1990s

The United States took action to lower carbon dioxide emissions and clean the atmosphere in the 1960s and 1970s with the Clean Air Act; however, it wasn't until the 1990s that a global effort to tackle the issue began. By that time, carbon emissions and the rising air temperature had created other challenges: a depleting ozone layer and climate change.

Climate change can most simply be defined as differing and accelerated weather-related events that make life on the planet difficult. For instance, climate change has been associated with warmer global temperatures, an increase in natural disasters, a loss of habitats, and a boost in greenhouse gases. There is no doubt that climate change is a serious issue. It has the potential to affect all life on Earth; however, since many changes occur over centuries or millennia, it's hard for people to see the issue as urgent. Still, modern scientists and others are working hard to make the planet better for future generations. This includes actions such as educating others, putting in place safeguards, lowering emissions, working with international agencies, and setting limits on carbon dioxide in the environment.

Ozone and Climate

People had been aware of threats to the environment years before a global climate initiative began in 1990. One of the contributors to climate change, **chlorofluorocarbons**, or CFCs, was confirmed in the late 1980s.

In 1985, scientist Joe Farman found a hole in the ozone layer over Antarctica. NASA satellites confirmed the presence of the hole, and it wasn't long before the issue was brought to the attention of the United Nations. The cause for the hole was

Conservation

Although lots of fossil fuels were being burned during the Industrial Revolution, people also cared about nature. In fact, since time and energy were freed up by new technology, people were more able to work to protect the environment.

People noticed that as time went on, the advancement of human society was having other effects on nature. Species were going extinct, natural resources were being used very rapidly, and places of natural beauty were being damaged. The industrial age saw a great increase in proponents of nature **preservation** and conservation. Some examples of organizations started later in this era are the United States Department of Agriculture (1862) and the US Forest Service (1905).

Other sources of public interest in conservation came from famous places like Yosemite, California. Writers like Horace Greeley and Thomas Starr King wrote at length about how beautiful the natural landscape was. Painters were also inspired by the untouched wilderness of Yosemite. Artists like Thomas Ayres, Thomas Moran, and Albert Bierstadt all created works inspired by Yosemite. These writers and artists helped spread awareness of Yosemite.

Landscape painters like Thomas Moran, whose work is shown here, inspired a growing interest in nature during the nineteenth century.

The works created by these individuals and others led to national efforts to protect the land. People responded to the beauty of nature and wanted to preserve it. The Yosemite National Park was established in 1890. In 1916, the National Park Service was created to oversee and protect national parks like Yosemite. To this day, the National Park Service works to educate people about nature preservation.

Greenhouse Effect

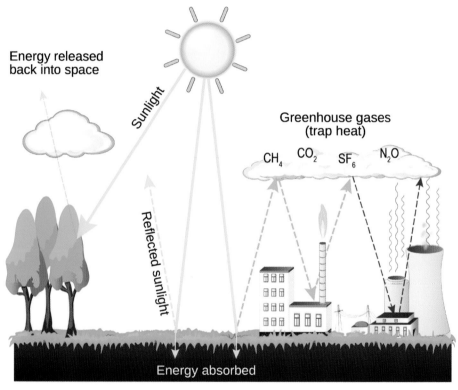

Energy released back into space

Sunlight

Greenhouse gases (trap heat)

CH_4 CO_2 SF_6 N_2O

Reflected sunlight

Energy absorbed

This image shows how greenhouse gases trap energy from the sun in Earth's atmosphere.

the presence of CFCs in Earth's atmosphere. Popularly used in the manufacturing of air conditioners and refrigerators, as well as a propellant in aerosol products such as hairspray and some cleaners, CFCs are a group of chemicals created to be inert and safe for humans. Unfortunately, as CFCs were used and released in normal manufacturing methods, they began to slowly integrate with higher portions of Earth's atmosphere. They began to deteriorate the ozone layer, a part of the atmosphere that protects all life on Earth from harmful **ultraviolet rays**. Although many CFCs aren't visibly damaging to people, at higher altitudes, they are exposed to ultraviolet rays, which break them down into chlorine and bromine atoms. These atoms collide with ozone atoms, breaking them apart and creating regular oxygen molecules that are not nearly as good at absorbing ultraviolet radiation as ozone atoms. Through this process, the hole in the atmosphere was created.

With the problem of the ozone layer in the public eye, people began to try to fix the problem. In September 1987, the Montreal Protocol on Substances That Deplete the Ozone Layer was established, identifying and regulating specific chemicals found to react with and deteriorate the ozone molecules that made up the ozone layer. The general plan was to phase the CFCs identified in the protocol out of use in manufacturing. Goals were set to reduce CFC emissions by 20 percent by 1994 and 50 percent by 1999. As scientific research continued, more ozone-harming CFCs were identified, and amendments to the Montreal Protocol were made. The London Protocol in 1990 identified more CFCs, as well as other chemicals also proven to break down ozone molecules. They set a deadline for total phaseout of the banned

President Roosevelt: Champion of Conservation

Born on October 27, 1858, Theodore Roosevelt was the son of Theodore Roosevelt Sr. and Martha Bulloch. Due to some health issues such as asthma, Roosevelt was educated at home for his early years. This gave him the opportunity to focus on his favorite subject: animals. With the help of a physical training regimen, Roosevelt's health would improve more and more, but he would not abandon his love for the wilderness.

In 1880, after graduating magna cum laude from Harvard, he went on to Columbia Law School. He eventually shifted his focus from law school to join the New York State Assembly, becoming the youngest person to serve as a representative. His political career skyrocketed over the course of a few years. He held various positions, including minority leader of the New York Assembly and captain of the National Guard. Unfortunately, his progress in politics was shaken by the tragic deaths of his mother and wife on the same day in 1884.

Rather than battle his emotions in the city, he decided to find solace in the South Dakota Territory. He stayed there for two years, working as a cattle rancher. In 1887, he founded the Boone and Crockett Club, an organization that works toward wildlife conservation to this day.

Upon returning to political life, Roosevelt ran for mayor of New York City but lost. Marrying his second wife, Edith, allowed him a respite from the defeat. It wasn't long before Roosevelt found different avenues to advance his career. Eventually, he

Theodore Roosevelt, smiling and waving to the crowd from his motorcade, circa 1910

President Roosevelt:
Champion of
Conservation (cont'd)

served as assistant secretary to the Navy. In 1898, Roosevelt resigned from that position and made a name for himself by organizing a volunteer cavalry group called the Rough Riders during the Spanish-American War. The Rough Riders made an impact in Cuba when they charged up San Juan Hill in 1898 during the Battle of San Juan Heights to assist in the seizure of San Juan Ridge. A few days later, the Spanish fleet fled Cuba, and the war ended shortly thereafter. Roosevelt was recommended for a Congressional Medal of Honor in recognition for his skill as a leader—but it wasn't awarded until 2001, eighty-two years after his death.

After a short term as governor from 1898 to 1901, Roosevelt was made US vice president under President William McKinley. Within a few months, McKinley was assassinated, and Roosevelt found himself president of the United States.

Roosevelt's time as president is best known for not only his opposition to business monopolies and his work to reform laws around labor and the workplace in America, but also his dedication to preserving the natural beauty of the American landscape as much as possible. In 1906, he signed the National Monuments Act, which allowed him to set aside many places, including the Grand Canyon, for federal protection. He also helped create several game reserves, wildlife sanctuaries, and national forests.

chemicals by the year 2000. Nearly one hundred countries agreed to the resolution.

Although these resolutions were instrumental in regulating the emissions of chemicals that were causing direct and immediate harm to the future of Earth's environment, the years following the enactments of the resolutions did not show progress right away. In February 1992, NASA satellites recorded abnormally high levels of **ozone-depleting chemicals** in the atmosphere above the United States. The organization warned that the ozone layer there could be depleted by as much as 40 percent if action was not taken. In 1995, the World Meteorological Association reported that the hole in the ozone layer was expanding more rapidly than previously believed. However, by that time, the levels of CFCs and other ozone-depleting chemicals in the atmosphere were showing measurable declines, proving that the regulations were at least having some effect.

As of 2017, the ozone layer has been showing signs of recovery, although the need for continued regulation of ozone-depleting substances and research into testing future chemicals for their reaction with ozone persists.

The IPCC

As concern for the atmosphere built in the 1980s, several international groups took action to fully understand the long-lasting implications associated with a damaged or changing climate. One of these was the Intergovernmental Panel on Climate Change (IPCC), created in 1988. Put in place by the World Meteorological Organization and the United Nations Environmental Program, its mission was to research and report findings on climate change. In 1990, just twenty years after the first celebration of Earth Day in 1970, the IPCC presented to

Rajendra Kumar Pachauri

Born in 1940 in Nainital, India, Rajendra Kumar Pachauri is a Nobel Peace Prize winner who acted as chairman of the Intergovernmental Panel on Climate Change from 2002 to 2015. Before he became head of the IPCC, Pachauri went to school in Lucknow, India, studying mechanical engineering. After briefly working in India for Diesel Locomotive Works, he continued his education in the United States at North Carolina State University. He finished with a master's degree and a PhD in 1974. After a few years working in universities in North Carolina and West Virginia, he returned to India. In 1982, he became the director of the Resources and Energy Institute. In 2001, he was appointed as a member of the Economic Advisory Council to the prime minister of India. In 2002, he became the head of the IPCC.

While leading the IPCC, Pachauri pushed for serious efforts to combat climate change. When interviewed by the AFP, a global news agency, about a proposed target of reducing atmospheric CO_2 levels to below 350 parts per million, Pachauri said, "As chairman of the IPCC, I cannot take a position because we do not make recommendations, but as a human being I am fully supportive of that goal. What is happening, and what is likely to happen, convinces me that the world must be really ambitious and very determined at moving toward a 350 target." Pachauri was awarded the Nobel Peace Prize in 2007 for his work with the IPCC. He retired from his position as head of the IPCC in 2015.

the United Nations a document called the First Assessment Report. It detailed scientific evidence for climate change, discussed issues associated with it, and highlighted its importance on an international scale. From there, the IPCC started to lay the foundation for helping countries in the United Nations collaborate on measuring, combating, and, with luck, reversing climate change.

Since its first report, the IPCC has provided regular updates on the status of climate change. They also play a key role in showing how nations should gather and share data related to climate change. This includes data like greenhouse gas emissions, climate measurements, and estimates based on current trends. Other reports from the IPCC were published in 1995, 2001, 2007, and a fifth report released in parts between 2013 and 2014. According to the IPCC's website, the next report is "expected to be finalized in 2022." As one of the leading authorities on climate change, the IPCC is expected to continue to be essential in present and future climate agreements.

fact!

Members of the UNFCCC treaty meet every year at the Conference of Parties (COP). Most of the meetings have been held in Bonn, Germany.

The UNFCCC

In 1992, the United Nations heeded the results of the First Assessment Report and set to work. Representatives from all over the world met at the Rio de Janeiro Earth Summit in June of that year. It was clear the world needed a treaty to help take

United Nations representatives stand and applaud the adoption of the Kyoto Protocol in 1997.

future action. The result was the United Nations Framework Convention on Climate Change (UNFCCC).

The UNFCCC went into effect in 1994. It had two main goals. The first and primary goal was to slow or reverse the effects of climate change, and to get nations to agree that climate change was a serious issue. The second goal was to lay the groundwork for how future treaties would work. The UNFCCC didn't have any calls to action or binding commitments for the parties who signed on. Instead, it paved the way for future treaties, which were to be referred to as "protocols," "agreements," or "accords."

Once the UNFCCC had finished laying the groundwork for future climate agreements, more than 150 nations signed the treaty.

Not long after the UNFCCC was finalized in 1994, work began on the first attempt at an international climate treaty. Borrowing tactics from the efforts to save the ozone layer in the 1980s, the new treaty was aimed to be ambitious and effective. With more than 150 nations having signed the UNFCCC, people thought the next step would be a shoo-in for success. This treaty was the Kyoto Protocol.

The Kyoto Protocol

Formed in Kyoto, Japan, in 1997, the Kyoto Protocol used guidelines established in the UNFCCC and set goals for reducing greenhouse gas emissions in industrialized, or developed, nations. The main goal for the protocol was for participating countries to reduce their greenhouse gas emissions to a little less than they were in 1990.

Because industrialized nations release more greenhouse gases, the protocol placed more burden on them to reduce their emissions. Developing nations, or nations with less industry and fewer greenhouse gas emissions, were also asked to take part, but to a lesser extent.

The protocol gave reduction targets for each country involved to meet by a certain date. In total, there were two commitment periods. From 2008 to 2012, their goal was to lower their greenhouse gas emissions by 5.5 percent from where they had been in 1990. In 2012, a second commitment period, from 2013 to 2020, was set.

In order for the protocol to pass, it needed fifty-five countries to sign it. Those countries also had to account for at least 55 percent of greenhouse gas emissions in the year 1990. Among them were India and Canada, bigger contributors of greenhouse gas emissions at the time. More than 150 nations agreed that the protocol was a good idea and adopted the treaty.

The Kyoto Protocol had strict rules about what would happen if a country didn't meet their goal in the first commitment period. Any such nation would be assigned a new goal in the second one. The second goal would be 30 percent more reductions, and the nation in trouble wouldn't be able to gain "credits" by helping other nations.

In 2001, with the start of the first commitment period less than a decade away, 178 nations met in Bonn, Germany, to sign and finalize the treaty. One notable absence was the United States. George W. Bush, the US president at the time, claimed that the steep goals of the protocol would cause economic problems for the country. Critics of the decision feared that Bush's ties to the fossil fuel industry influenced his decision to stop supporting the protocol. Thus, the United States dropped out of the treaty, joining Sudan and Afghanistan as the only nations in the United Nations not to commit to the final protocol's terms.

The loss of support from the United States was a significant setback for the protocol. Without it, the protocol might not have enough **signatories** to pass. Some hope for the plan was restored, however, when Russia committed to the treaty in 2004. The treaty went into effect in 2005, and much of the international community seemed poised to tackle climate change.

Facing Challenges

The Kyoto Protocol had a significant obstacle during its first commitment period. Because the United States was not participating and China was made exempt from the protocol, they were not required to make any changes. This was a problem because the United States and China were the largest contributors of greenhouse gases in the world. This led Canada to officially renounce the protocol in 2011, claiming that the treaty was unrealistic if the United States and China weren't going to help. In 2012, at the end of the first commitment period, it was clear that there was more work to be done.

In 2012, in Doha, Qatar, the Kyoto Protocol was updated with the new list of committed countries, a new list of greenhouse gases to track and regulate, and a new commitment period set to end in 2020. With more time, more nations on board, and better information, some believed that the Kyoto Protocol might have what it needed to succeed. However, further lack of support from the United States caused some nations to lose faith in the treaty. Multiple nations began to call for a new agreement to fix the problems of the previous one. In 2016, they would have their answer.

2

From Kyoto to Paris

As support for the Kyoto Protocol began to dwindle, it became clear that the international community needed a new agreement. Many believed that the Kyoto Protocol was going to expire with few, if any, goals met. Although it did not seem like much progress was made with the agreement, the need for action remained the same. In order to attempt to correct some important issues, the new agreement needed to find a way to ensure the top producers of greenhouse gases were on board. The goals and burdens placed on each nation needed to be reasonable, and above all, cooperation needed to remain a priority.

In 2015, work began on the first drafts of the next step in fighting climate change on an international level. The new accord, designed to start when the Kyoto Protocol expired in 2020, was designed using the same ground rules established by the UNFCCC. However, newer tactics allowing individual

Opposite: UNESCO (Paris headquarters pictured here) works closely with the United Nations to protect important spaces in the world.

International leaders celebrate the completion of the Paris Agreement on December 12, 2015.

nations to set their own goals were made part of the accord. After a month of drafting, the Paris Climate Agreement, or the Paris Climate Accord, was born.

Passing the Paris Climate Agreement

The Paris Climate Agreement, or simply the Paris Agreement, was finalized and made available for countries to sign in the spring of 2016. In order to pass, it needed at least fifty-five nations who were part of the UNFCCC treaty to sign. As with the Kyoto Protocol, those fifty-five nations needed to account for at least 55 percent of greenhouse gas emissions.

Unlike the Kyoto Protocol, there was less worry that the agreement might not pass. In the end, 195 countries signed the treaty, signaling that almost every single country in the United Nations wanted to take part in the accord. Even parties that had been exempt from the Kyoto Protocol signed. Crucially, the United States also signed. It seemed that the world was moving in the right direction.

The First Two Countries That Didn't Sign

In order to take part in the Paris Agreement, countries had to be on the UNFCCC treaty. There are some nations and groups in the UN that are interested in the Paris Agreement but can't sign until they join the UNFCCC. One example of this is the **Holy See**. It is an observer state on the UNFCCC but not a signing member. Of the UNFCCC members, only two nations did not sign the Paris Climate Agreement initially: Nicaragua and Syria.

Nicaragua didn't sign because its leaders felt the agreement didn't have enough force. The Kyoto Protocol had a system for setting steeper goals for countries that failed to meet their targets.

Ban Ki-Moon: Secretary-General of the UN

Ban Ki-moon was the secretary-general for the United Nations from 2007 to 2016. As the eighth person to hold the position, he was a firm advocate for various challenges facing the world. During his time in office, he worked to draw international attention to issues like access to safe water sources, energy policies, and climate change. He also worked to support poorer countries and fought for gender equality and women's rights.

Born in South Korea in 1944, Ban grew up during the Korean War in the early 1950s. The conflict and its aftereffects had a great impact on his life. He was quoted on his biography page for the United Nations website on the topic: "I grew up in war and saw the United Nations help my country to recover and rebuild. That experience was a big part of what led me to pursue a career in public service. As Secretary-General, I am determined to see this organization deliver tangible, meaningful results that advance peace, development and human rights."

Shortly after his election in 2007, Ban set up the 2007 Climate Change Summit meeting, which helped renew efforts to fight climate change in the wake of the Kyoto Protocol. When he was up for reelection in 2011, he received a

Ban Ki-moon speaks at a press conference in December 2016.

unanimous vote. He is credited with making the United Nations more transparent and effective. He was also instrumental in the foundation and success of the Paris Agreement's focus on aiding poorer countries. He retired in 2016 at the end of his second term.

targets. The Paris Agreement is more of a promise to try, but there's no mechanism in the agreement to punish a country not doing its part. Representatives from Nicaragua had stated that the country will set its own goals; however, in September 2017, they announced they would join the agreement.

At the time of the agreement's introduction, Syria had been in a civil war since 2011—a main reason why few expected it to take part in the agreement. However, Syria could later choose to sign that or any other future agreement under the UNFCCC. Together, Nicaragua and Syria accounted for less than 1 percent of global greenhouse gas emissions. While every contribution counts, lack of participation from Nicaragua or Syria wasn't a danger to the Paris Agreement's chances of passing.

Withdrawal from the Accord

One of the biggest obstacles that faced the Kyoto Protocol was the lack of support from the United States. The United States's absence from the protocol almost meant it didn't pass. Although the United States did sign the Paris Agreement initially, changes in US politics in 2017 raised the question of US withdrawal from it. Eventually, that question was answered when US president Donald Trump officially announced the United States' withdrawal from the agreement on June 1, 2017.

If a country wants to withdraw from the agreement, they can do so, but only after it has been in effect for three years. Since the Paris Agreement was put into force in 2016, any country wishing to drop out has to wait until 2019. Since national goals are voluntary, any country waiting to drop out isn't forced by the agreement to contribute in the meantime. However, dropping out of an agreement supported by almost two hundred nations could—and has—caused tension.

Goals of the Agreement

Countries who signed the Paris Agreement were agreeing to work toward three main goals. These goals were listed in Article 2 of the agreement. The first was to try to stop the global average temperature from rising by 2 degrees Celsius, or 3.6 degrees Fahrenheit, above pre-industrial levels. They also agreed that if at all possible, the temperature rise should be kept below 1.5°C (2.7°F). The second goal was to work toward finding ways to adapt to the changing climate in the meantime. One of the main priorities for this goal was preserving Earth's food supply. The third and final goal was to encourage businesses to invest in technologies and practices that reduce greenhouse gas emissions.

fact!

Another effect of climate change is rising sea levels. The IPCC and NASA predict that sea levels could rise between 0.2 and 2 meters (0.6 and 6.5 feet) if greenhouse gas levels aren't slowed or reduced.

In order to meet these goals, countries that signed the accord agreed to reduce their greenhouse gas emissions. Article 4, paragraph 1 of the agreement states, "In order to achieve the long-term temperature goal set out in Article 2, Parties aim to reach global peaking of greenhouse gas emissions as soon as possible."

The agreement aims to reach its goals by having nations set their own targets for reducing emissions. These are called "nationally determined contributions," or NDCs. Countries determined their NDCs during a conference that took place in winter of 2015. Nations that signed the agreement were agreeing to set clear, public goals and promising to work to meet them. Countries taking part in the agreement were also promising to set goals that actually mattered. A giant country with the most greenhouse gas emissions couldn't slack off by setting purposely low goals. Also, if a country hit its target for reducing emissions, the next target would need to be higher. If one country helped another reduce their emissions, that could count toward its own goal, too.

Although reducing greenhouse gas emissions and slowing the rise in global temperature was the main focus of the accord, the Paris Agreement mentioned other things countries could do. Article 5 brought up ways to deal with greenhouse gases already in the atmosphere: "Parties should take action to conserve and enhance, as appropriate, sinks and reservoirs of greenhouse gases as referred to in Article 4, paragraph 1 (d), of the Convention, including forests." Plants naturally absorb carbon dioxide, using it with sunlight, water, and nutrients in the ground to sustain themselves. By preserving and growing areas with lots of plant life, carbon dioxide in the atmosphere can be naturally reduced.

Article 5 also mentioned that countries could encourage groups and individuals to make progress through incentives. Tax benefits, funding, and other rewards could encourage businesses and other groups to help. By doing so, new technologies and techniques for preserving and enhancing the environment could make a big difference.

The Rules of Working Together

Article 6 of the Paris Agreement discussed the rules for countries working together to meet their goals. Countries were encouraged to share techniques, technology, and policy ideas to help each other. After all, if a country discovered a radical new method for reducing greenhouse gas emissions, sharing it with the rest of the world would benefit everyone. However, the country getting help would need to still try to meet their goals independently as

This scene from the film *The Day After Tomorrow* shows dramatically rising water levels and flooding.

well, through other means. They couldn't use help from others as proof they were making progress.

Another important part of the agreement focused on the economic impact of working together. Countries in the accord had to keep in mind that some countries were much poorer than others. If one of the most developed countries in the world invented a new product reducing their emissions, not all countries would be able to buy that product. Parties to the agreement were encouraged to find "nonmarket approaches" to help other countries without making poverty in those countries worse. One way to do this was to share methods so that countries could develop their own versions of that product. Another way was to have both public organizations and private businesses work together in the country needing help.

fact!

The Cancun Adaptation Framework is an agreement passed in 2010 during a UN Climate Change Conference. Parties agreed that adaptation to a changing climate is just as important as trying to mitigate the changes.

Preparing for the Future

The Paris Agreement recognized that the changes countries needed to make would take time. The international community learned from the ozone crisis of the 1980s that even if countries met all their goals, the climate could get worse before it got better. In the meantime, members of the Paris Agreement recognized the need to be ready for that to happen. Article 7 of the Paris Agreement focused on this topic.

It set the goals of "enhancing adaptive capacity, strengthening resilience and reducing vulnerability to climate change."

As part of the Paris Agreement, countries agreed to cooperate to adapt to the changing environment. The agreement suggested different methods to cooperate and adapt. For instance, countries could share information and notes about their various adaptation attempts, and learn from each other. They could also share scientific knowledge and methods to help each other make more informed decisions.

As the climate changes, natural resources, weather patterns, and even land geography can be affected. Just like with reducing greenhouse gases, countries are encouraged to work together to adapt and prepare for future changes in Earth's environment. Particular attention should be paid to helping countries who are either unable to adapt, have resources at risk in a changing climate, or both. The agreement also recognized that certain groups in a society might need more help adapting. For example, poor people living on a coastline might need more help adapting to rising water levels than other people with more money.

Preparing for the effects of climate change is important. However, such preparations take time and require resources. The accord encouraged countries to focus on mitigating the effects of climate change. This could slow the need for new adaptations and also reduce the costs necessary to make and improve existing adaptations. Just like with greenhouse gas reductions, countries in the Paris Agreement were expected to keep others informed about their progress.

Other Mechanisms of the Agreement

The Paris Agreement is a large and comprehensive environmental agreement that covers many issues related to climate change, such as damage to resources. However, a lot of the mechanisms that the Paris Agreement uses to accomplish its goals are smaller agreements under the UNFCCC. These smaller parts of the UNFCCC treaty were made after the Kyoto Protocol and are part of the Paris Agreement today.

As Earth's climate changes, weather patterns will change. Many scientists predict that severe weather conditions will become more frequent. Droughts, floods, storms, and sudden drops in temperature can all cause damage to different places around the world. In order to prepare for such situations, the Warsaw International Mechanism for Loss and Damage Associated with Climate Change Impacts was established in 2013. It would be managed by an executive committee, who would help nations prepare for and prevent damage caused by climate change, including damage that occurs slowly over time, as well as assessing the damage that occured. They would also coordinate efforts to help countries and areas recover from damage caused by climate change.

The UNFCCC's Financial Mechanism was established in Durban, South Africa, in 2011. The mechanism tasks one or more international entities with investing money in projects and technologies to help the Paris Agreement and other future accords meet their goals. The two main groups tasked with performing this mechanism are the Global Environment Facility and the Green Climate Fund.

The Technology Mechanism of the UNFCCC was created in 2010 in Cancun, Mexico, to help developing countries obtain and use technologies that can help them adapt and prepare for a changing climate. A Technology Executive Committee, made up of twenty technology experts from countries around the world, aims to develop and share technologies in keeping with the goals of the UNFCCC and the Paris Agreement.

Protecting Developing Nations

Many of the goals of the Paris Agreement mention helping developing countries. Developing countries are nations that have less industry and smaller economies than industrial nations like the United States and the United Kingdom. Developed nations have the most ability to cause harm through climate change since they burn more fossil fuels. Developing nations have less ability to protect themselves from damages and dangers caused by climate change. Poorer nations won't be able to afford a solution to climate change if it's too expensive. Smaller countries won't be able to use solutions that require huge areas of untouched forestland. Parties to the Paris Agreement agreed that developing nations would need help dealing with climate change.

Because each country in the Paris Agreement gets to set its own goals for contribution, each country might prioritize itself over others. Allowing countries to help each other with new technology and practices is one way to stop that. However, the Paris Agreement specifically encouraged developed nations to help poorer nations and not just their economic neighbors. The agreement specifically encouraged developed nations to offer funding for nations most vulnerable to the effects of climate change. Examples in Article 9 included small nations with less space for forestland and island nations with no room for expansion.

Tracking Progress and Informing Others

Countries taking part in the Paris Agreement had a big task ahead of them. Slowing the progress of climate change was challenging

Christiana Figueres: Executive Secretary of the UNFCCC

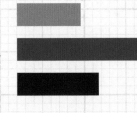

Christiana Figueres is a Costa Rican diplomat who had key influence on the Paris Agreement and other major parts of the UNFCCC. Under Figueres's supervision, the climate change conferences from 2010 to 2016 created the Green Climate Fund, the Cancun Adaptation Mechanism, the Warsaw International Mechanism, and the Technology Mechanism of the UNFCCC.

Born in Costa Rica in 1956, Figueres grew up in San José. After attending Swarthmore College in Pennsylvania, she earned a master's degree in social anthropology from the London School of Economics in 1981. In 1997, she began work as a representative of Costa Rica to the United Nations. After the UN failed to pass a climate accord in Copenhagen, Denmark, in 2010, Figueres was appointed as the UNFCCC's executive secretary. During her time in office, she helped organize six climate change conferences, leading to the establishment of key parts of the Paris Agreement.

Christiana Figueres at a climate summit in Paris, France, in 2015

Figueres is known for helping establish rules on **deforestation** with regard to climate change. She is also recognized for her understanding of the role of developing nations in climate change agreements. She has worked to raise awareness of human rights issues around the world. In 2016, she was selected to be Costa Rica's official candidate for the office of secretary-general of the United Nations.

Not only did Figueres help shape the UNFCCC and the Paris Agreement, but she conducted significant work outside the UN. She made special efforts to meet with groups to encourage them to take part in fighting climate change.

enough, but there were other duties, too. All of Article 12 was devoted to the need for parties involved in the agreement to educate and inform people about climate change. If people didn't know about or didn't understand climate change, they couln't help, and could cause more harm. Parties were also encouraged to try to get people to take part in fighting climate change. One of the best ways to get people involved is to make information about climate change easy to find and easy to read. The texts of the Paris Agreement and the Kyoto Protocol were made freely available online. They were also translated into multiple languages to reach more people.

Countries in the Paris Agreement had other information goals, too. They were required to provide two very important pieces of information. The first was a regular update on the amount of greenhouse gases the country created and removed. This information had to comply with standards set by the IPCC. It also needed to be gathered using methods that the IPCC and other parties to the agreement considered accurate. The second was the ability to compare the first piece with other reports over time. This could show the progress of a country in meeting its goals.

Every year, members of the UNFCCC treaty met and exchanged information. This gave countries the chance to officially update others. Under the agreement, countries reported news about advances in technology to fight and adapt to climate change. Developing countries also gave news about any growth in their ability to help. Countries that were part of the UNFCCC but not the Paris Agreement could attend these meetings. However, they could not vote on decisions about the Paris Agreement.

Although members of the UNFCCC met regularly, the Paris Agreement had another rule that parties agreed to follow. They agreed to have another meeting in 2023 to see how progress toward fighting climate change was going. This meeting is called the "global stocktake." One will take place every five years after the first one. During the global stocktake, countries will exchange more information and review their goals and progress. The global stocktake meeting will mark the start of a new term for the Paris Agreement, much like the Kyoto Protocol's commitment period terms.

Taking Measurements

The first step toward reducing emissions is measuring the atmosphere. Without knowing how much carbon dioxide, methane, and other greenhouse gases are in the air, it's hard to tell if any action is having an impact. However, by capturing samples of the air and studying it, scientists can track any changes in the atmosphere's composition. NASA and other organizations study Earth's atmosphere and determine how much carbon dioxide and other greenhouse gases are in Earth's atmosphere at any given time. By doing this, it's possible to predict trends and changes in the atmosphere's composition and prepare for any significant, globally reaching changes.

The Earth System Research Laboratory (ESRL) is a group that has been collecting measurements of Earth's atmosphere for decades. The ESRL does this by taking samples of the air using planes, ships, and various collection sites around the world. Because the process is as simple as capturing some air in a container, collecting and calculating data can happen daily. By measuring the amount of carbon dioxide in each sample and comparing current and past sample data, the ESRL can track greenhouse gas levels in the atmosphere over time.

The ESRL runs its Global Monitoring Division out of its main observatory station in Mauna Loa, Hawaii. The Global Monitoring Division is responsible for conducting tests, making calculating, and cooperating with other atmospheric observatory stations all over the world.

One of the provisions of the Kyoto Protocol was that countries that had more greenhouse gas emissions should reduce their emissions more than other countries with fewer emissions. However, it's not so easy to measure exactly how much carbon dioxide, methane, or other greenhouse gases an entire country produces. People, cars, and cows don't come with emissions meters on them, after all. However, by measuring how much fossil fuel and other resources a nation uses, it's possible to calculate emission levels. One of the main groups calculating emissions levels this way is the World Resources Institute.

The World Resources Institute (WRI) is an international organization that was founded in 1982. According to the WRI website, "WRI's mission is to move human society to live in ways that protect Earth's environment and its capacity to provide for the needs and aspirations of current and future generations." The WRI works with scientists, economists, and other experts all over the world to measure the climate, research cleaner sources of energy, and preserve natural resources.

Possible Obstacles

While the Paris Agreement aimed to do a lot, there are still things that could pose as challenges to its progress. Even with the combined efforts of more than one hundred nations, these obstacles are still worth understanding.

Much of the Paris Agreement was about the goals countries had in the agreement. Countries got to set their own greenhouse-gas reduction goals. They got to set their own adaptation goals. They got to set their own goals for helping other countries, too. But what would happen if a country in the accord set a goal and didn't meet it?

Unlike the Kyoto Protocol, the Paris Agreement didn't have any sort of consequence for countries that didn't follow through. The Kyoto Protocol took the previous, failed goal for one term and increased it by 30 percent for the next term. This was a punishment in multiple ways. In order to meet the new goal, countries in the Kyoto Protocol would have to take more drastic action—which might have had negative effects on that nation's economy. The Paris Agreement, on the other hand, didn't require punitive consequences. Instead, countries that were part of the Paris Agreement were promising to meet their goals. The only "punishment" for failure was that climate change continued to occur. This put everyone in danger, not just the country in question.

One country not meeting a goal may also affect the attitudes of other nations. If a country in the accord appeared to be willfully ignoring the agreement for some reason, other nations would notice. In this case, other countries might change the way they interacted with the offending nation. This could affect diplomatic relations, international trade, and other areas where nations interacted with the offending country.

Another possibility was the failure of the Paris Agreement to meet its overall goal: lowering global temperature. If the global average temperature increased beyond the few degrees set out by the accord, a few things could happen. For one, the Paris Agreement might be modified, with new goals. It's also possible that a new agreement with different rules might take its place. The future of the Paris Agreement will become clearer with the 2023 global stocktake meeting.

3

Beyond Kyoto and Paris

The passing of the Kyoto Protocol and the Paris Agreement were clear messages from the United Nations: Earth needs help. People must act now, and they must work together. Both the Kyoto Protocol and the Paris Agreement had far-reaching effects on people around the world. They emphasized the need to reduce greenhouse gas emissions. In doing so, they also accelerated the development of **alternative energy** sources, like wind, solar, and hydroelectric. They brought global attention to the issue of climate change. They encouraged governments, businesses, and individual citizens to take action. Many of the actions and practices that occur in societies around the globe have been changed in part by these international agreements.

Reactions to Kyoto

The Kyoto Protocol was one of the first attempts at a multinational agreement on climate change. It emphasized a strong need to

Opposite: Wind turbines, pictured here, are blown by the wind and use that energy to make electricity.

specifically reduce the emission of greenhouse gases. However, the idea of emissions regulation wasn't entirely new. The ozone crisis of the late 1980s showed that it was possible to regulate emissions. It also showed that industries could make changes without damaging the economy too much. With the help of the internet and television, lots of people knew about the Kyoto Protocol.

Reactions to the Kyoto Protocol were mixed. Lots of people liked the idea of taking action to protect the planet. Many leaders of industrialized nations were optimistic about the agreement. US president Bill Clinton commented that he felt that the Kyoto Protocol was both "environmentally sound and economically stable." However, some groups criticized the protocol. Some environmentalists worried that the Kyoto Protocol might not be strong enough to make a difference in time. They felt the need for strong and fast action to protect the planet as soon as possible. Some business leaders thought that the protocol was too strong. They felt that eliminating fossil fuel energies was too expensive to do in so little time.

In the summer of 2001, the time came for countries to sign the final version of the Kyoto Protocol. However, the United States did not take part. Just a few months before the deadline, the United States had elected a new president. President George W. Bush felt that the Kyoto Protocol would cause economic problems for the country. He also felt the protocol didn't ask for enough contribution from developing countries around the world. In the end, he decided not to commit the country to the protocol. Instead, Bush passed policies to slow the growth of emission rates, but not reduce them. The loss of support from the United States was a big problem for the UN. People thought this meant the Kyoto Protocol might not pass. Even if it did, people worried that the United States' actions could counteract the efforts of other nations.

Despite the setback caused by the United States' rejection of the protocol, people still got to work. The Kyoto Protocol started the process toward many of the changes the Paris Agreement would help make. Although the United States wasn't required to do anything, many groups still set out to reduce greenhouse gas emissions. Businesses, universities, and communities all over the world started trying to "go green."

Reactions to Paris

The Paris Agreement, like the Kyoto Protocol, was a big deal for the United Nations. With the support of nearly every nation in the UNFCCC, people were more hopeful than ever that it would succeed. Initial reactions to the Paris Agreement were similar to those for the Kyoto Protocol. Some felt it was not strong enough, while others felt it would cause too much economic harm. Some people didn't like the fact that the Paris Agreement didn't punish countries for not meeting their goals. Others felt that countries being allowed to set their own goals might allow them to be lazy about contributing. Many people felt that the Paris Agreement was at least a step in the right direction. All of the world's top producers of greenhouse gases signed the Paris Agreement, which came into force in November 2016.

History sometimes has a way of repeating itself. Just as the Kyoto Protocol was disrupted by a newly elected US president, the Paris Agreement faced a similar issue. In June 2017, US president Donald Trump announced that his country would leave the Paris Agreement. Many world leaders were disappointed by this, but others were resolute to continue without the United

States. Moreover, some state governments within the United States promised to try to meet goals of their own.

Declining Fossil Fuels and New and Different Energy Sources

In the twentieth and twenty-first centuries, the widespread use of fossil fuels has become a double-edged sword for human societies around the world. The wide availability of fossil fuels has made them cheap and effective sources of energy for decades. Businesses developed around the collection, refinement, and use of fossil fuels, creating jobs and economic growth. However, burning fossil fuels remains the largest contributor to climate change and the rise in global average temperature.

Fossil fuels have seen a cycle of dominance followed by replacement throughout history. Since all fossil fuels take millions of years to form naturally, humans have almost always used them faster than they could be made. This means that over time, one fossil fuel was often replaced by the next one when it became cheaper and easier to get.

During the industrial age, the primary fossil fuel was coal. Today, the primary fossil fuel used for energy is crude oil, also known as petroleum. Crude oil is used to make gasoline and other fuels, as well as some plastics. Like coal, crude oil is found underground and is formed over millions of years by the pressure on the remains of dead plants and animals buried under Earth's crust. Because crude oil, like coal, takes millions of years to be made, the consumption of fossil fuels will eventually reduce as fossil fuels become more and more scarce. Even today, shortages and rising prices due to smaller supplies and more effort needed to extract fossil fuels are the result of fossil-fuel scarcity. However,

Crude oil looks like this before it's refined into other substances.

the amount of greenhouse gases released by the burning of fossil fuels is enough to cause severe harm to Earth's environment. Like coal, crude oil can be dangerous to collect. Oil is flammable, and the machinery used to drill and collect it can cause severe injury or worse to oil workers.

Another fossil fuel widely used today is natural gas, a flammable gas found underground and captured using similar technologies and processes to crude oil and coal. It is composed mostly of methane and is considered by many to be a "cleaner" fossil fuel than oil or coal, due to the fact that burning it produces less greenhouse gas than burning oil. However, natural gas, like other fossil fuels, takes a very long time to be made naturally. Likewise, its supply is not infinite. It will eventually run out as consumption rises. Because fossil fuels create greenhouse gases when burned, the need for new, safer, alternative energies has grown over time.

The Kyoto Protocol and Paris Agreement have had a positive impact on the alternative energies industry. Alternative energy sources like wind power, solar power, and hydropower have become viable fossil fuel replacements. In the years after the passing of both agreements, interest in alternative energy sources grew. Time and technological development make alternative energies better and cheaper every year. Alternative energy sources carry many benefits today, despite their current limits, such as cost and quantity. The primary benefit for most of them is a vast reduction in greenhouse gas emissions. With enough research, development, production, and affordability, the need for fossil fuels as an energy source might one day be phased out entirely.

Energies on the Rise

Over the years, various methods for gathering these alternative energies have been developed. For instance, wind power is captured by large windmills, or turbines. Solar power is captured by **photovoltaic panels** like solar panels. Hydropower is often captured by waterwheels or dams. Over time, these technologies have become more efficient and cheaper to install. Each alternative form of energy has its own strengths and weaknesses. It is important to note, though, that many weaknesses are diminishing as time goes on.

One of the most promising areas of development in alternative energy is solar power. Photovoltaic

fact!

The first photovoltaic cell capable of generating electricity was created in 1839 by physicist Alexandre-Edmond Becquerel. Since its discovery, using light to generate power has become less and less expensive over time.

solar panels are placed facing the sky. They convert the light emitted by the sun into electricity. Because the sun is unaffected by the gathering of solar energy and it will last for millions of years to come, solar power generation is seen as a free, almost limitless source of energy, if it can be harnessed efficiently. Technology for solar panels is constantly evolving, making solar energy more and more viable and profitable for businesses and industries to invest in. Solar energy faces some obstacles, however. Clouds and other weather patterns can limit how much sunlight a solar panel can collect. It also takes a lot of solar panels in a wide space to be efficient, and that land or space could be used for other purposes like growing food or housing. However, putting solar panels on rooftops of buildings and homes can help reduce power costs.

Wind is another source of naturally occurring energy. Wind turbines have been used to collect clean energy for decades, but like other power-generation methods, they have their downsides. Currently, each individual wind turbine doesn't provide much

This solar energy farm has rows of solar panels converting light from the sun into electricity.

energy, so wind turbines are used in great numbers in larger areas. Much like solar panels, this takes up space that could be used for other purposes. Likewise, the wind turbines are very tall and can mar a beautiful landscape.

Hydroelectric dams, although seemingly less problematic for the environment, still have significant effects on the lands upstream and downstream from where the dam is placed. Dams often mean that the land downriver has somewhat less water, and lands upriver are often flooded as the water builds up against the dam. This can cause problems both for animals that live on or near the lands around the dam and for people settled along rivers upstream or downstream who face drought or flooding from the change in water level.

Geothermal energy is another possibility. It comes from harnessing heat from hot water or hot rock located miles beneath Earth's surface. However, the process of harnessing geothermal energy takes a lot of water. It is expensive to start a geothermal generation project. It also requires a lot of digging, which is difficult to do in areas already packed with buildings.

Nuclear energy is another source of energy that has strengths and weaknesses. One positive is that it doesn't release greenhouse gases. The materials used in nuclear power generation are naturally occurring and plentiful. Although nuclear energy generates a lot of electricity inexpensively, it has a lot of dangers. Nuclear generators use radioactive materials to create heat, which is then harnessed for energy. To keep things from overheating, water is used to cool things down. When water gets too hot, it boils and becomes steam. To keep the water from boiling as easily, nuclear generators use large chambers to keep the water under pressure. Although scientists are working on new methods of cooling, water is still much cheaper and more widely available for current

The Prairie Island nuclear power plant is located in Redwing, Minnesota.

nuclear plants. Because of the high pressures and large sizes of nuclear facilities, accidents can have major consequences. Nuclear meltdowns can release dangerous radiation, nuclear waste, and irradiated dust for miles. This can cause radiation poisoning for humans and contribute to many kinds of cancers.

Nuclear power generators also create radioactive waste, which takes thousands of years to degrade naturally and is very dangerous to people. Currently, the only means people have to remove radioactive waste is just setting it aside and waiting for a better solution. Although some theorize that enough nuclear reactors could provide energy for everyone, nuclear reactors are big and expensive. They also take a long time to build, and with the dangers associated with radioactive waste and the risk of meltdowns, people don't want nuclear plants near where they live. Perhaps in the future, if nuclear power becomes safer and causes less waste, it might be more of a viable alternative.

Technological Changes

The Paris Agreement specifically mentions that new technologies are needed to help protect Earth. It's clear we need technologies to fight climate change. We also need technologies to help us adapt to the coming changes. Many of the changes in technology encouraged by the Paris Agreement are already starting to happen.

fact!

One of the most famous nuclear reactor meltdown catastrophes was the Chernobyl disaster, which took place in Ukraine in 1986. Another famous meltdown occurred in Fukushima, Japan, in 2011, when an earthquake damaged the Fukushima nuclear plant.

Dr. Steven Chu: Clean Energy Expert

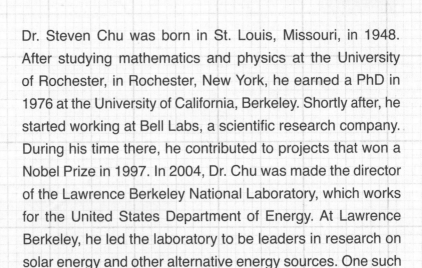

Dr. Steven Chu was born in St. Louis, Missouri, in 1948. After studying mathematics and physics at the University of Rochester, in Rochester, New York, he earned a PhD in 1976 at the University of California, Berkeley. Shortly after, he started working at Bell Labs, a scientific research company. During his time there, he contributed to projects that won a Nobel Prize in 1997. In 2004, Dr. Chu was made the director of the Lawrence Berkeley National Laboratory, which works for the United States Department of Energy. At Lawrence Berkeley, he led the laboratory to be leaders in research on solar energy and other alternative energy sources. One such project is the Helios Research Project. It aims to use solar energy to create clean fuel sources from sunlight.

In 2009, he was appointed secretary of energy for the United States. During his time in office, Dr. Chu continued to conduct research and publish scientific papers. He also worked to regulate dangerous practices in gathering natural gas. Dr. Chu was a firm advocate for reducing the use of fossil fuels in favor of cleaner energies. He resigned from the Department of Energy in 2013 and resumed working in scientific research at Stanford University. At the end of his time as secretary of energy, he wrote a letter to the Department of Energy. In the letter, he emphasized the need for work to continue improving clean energy sources: "As the saying goes, the Stone Age did not end because we ran out of stones; we transitioned to better solutions."

The Paris Agreement has affected the transportation industry and challenged companies to create new vehicle designs. A lot of the fossil fuels in use today are used to power vehicles. Cars and trucks have become very commonplace for many countries all over the world. People rely on the ability to travel long distances quickly for their jobs. Being able to deliver large amounts of goods with trucks is vital to people who need them. Transportation technology is adapting to regulations from treaties and other environmental bodies by eliminating the use of fossil fuels to run vehicles. Several designs for zero-emissions vehicles are in the works, with electric cars being one of the most popular and already accessible options. Electric vehicles are becoming more powerful, more efficient, and more affordable every year. Because they don't use **combustible fuels**, they're also safer. However, until electric vehicles become cheaper and more convenient than gasoline-powered vehicles, gas-powered cars will be around.

Other changes to technology include improving the technology used to study Earth. Satellites have been used to study weather since 1960. However, more precise tools and technologies are developed every year that help us understand more about the planet. Thermal images from NASA provided one of the first incentives to solving the ozone crisis. Computers capable of predicting where storms are headed help people prepare and prevent damage. These tools will become more necessary as climate change continues to affect the environment.

Technology is also adapting for climate change with regards to drinking water. As droughts begin to occur more frequently, access to clean, fresh water is harder to get. This is especially true in developing countries. Lack of clean water can lead to the spread of disease as well as dehydration. Technologies are being developed to handle situations like this. For instance, water filters capable of eliminating bacteria and diseases can help make some sources of water drinkable. Other systems of gathering and reserving water from rainfall can help, too.

Protecting Natural Resources

One of the biggest dangers of climate change is its effect on Earth's natural resources. The Kyoto and Paris accords have both had great influence on how countries manage their resources. Trees are a good example of this. They are used for lumber to construct buildings and other structures, but trees also absorb carbon dioxide. To help fight climate change, more countries are stopping or reducing deforestation. They are planting trees to replace those being cut down. This preserves a resource and also helps fight climate change.

One goal mentioned specifically in the Paris Agreement is the preservation of food sources. As the climate changes, more food sources will be at risk. Changes in weather patterns, temperature, moisture, and air and soil quality can all occur due to climate change. These changes can have a negative impact on the various food sources people rely on or enjoy. The need to adapt has given rise to new methods in agriculture.

This Tesla Model S electric car charges at a car-charging station.

Save the Bees!

Anyone who has ever been stung by one of these yellow-and-black insects might not be the biggest fan of one of nature's most important, hard-working, buzzing critters. After all, they do gather in great numbers, and each one has the ability to deliver a painful sting. A single sting could also be dangerous for those who are allergic. However, bees play a vital role in agriculture, and they are at risk of damage from climate change.

Not only do bees help wild plants grow and reproduce, but they're also often used to pollinate crops for farmers. Apple orchards, for example, sometimes keep **apiaries** to have bees help pollinate the apple trees as well as to collect their honey. Climate change, however, is having its own impact on honeybees, which face myriad problems already. Widespread use of pesticides has made it hard for bees to gather nectar safely.

Some of the greatest risks for damage to bees come from risks to plants, and not the bees themselves. As the global average temperature rises due to greenhouse gas emissions, plants can be "fooled" by a few days of warmer weather into budding at a time when a cold evening can kill the buds. Not only does this mean that the plant is much less likely to flower, but it means that the flower's nectar isn't there for bees to collect and turn into honey, or pick up pollen to pass to the other plants. This poses a problem both for plants that play an important role in Earth's environment and to apiarists around the world, who rely on honey and beeswax as a portion of their income.

Today, bees play important roles in helping flowers and fruits grow.
Here, a bee perches on a lavender flower.

The Gros Michel banana once was popular in grocery stores. However, it became infected by diseases and was replaced by the Cavendish.

Preserving Our Food Supply

Agriculture is a constantly evolving field with a long history of adapting to new needs. In the 1930s, farmers in the United States received a hard lesson in the need to adapt. Droughts and winds combined with poor care of farmland caused dust storms to rage across prairies in North America. Farmers had to use new methods for keeping dirt fertile for crops and on the ground. The Kyoto and Paris treaties have influenced the rise of other adaptations in agriculture.

One of the biggest areas of development for adapting agriculture is the need for more efficiency. As populations grow, space available for farming shrinks. Each acre of farmland will need to be able to produce more food. Crops will also need to be able to withstand the coming effects of climate change. One way food growers are researching how to improve efficiency is through indoor growing. Growing in enclosed spaces can allow for more control over the growing process. Greenhouses today can control how often plants get watered, how much sunlight they receive, and the composition of the soil and air the plants grow in. With the help of the right technology, it's even possible that future farms might have multiple levels.

Another way plants are being adapted today is through **genetically modified organisms**, or GMOs. There are two kinds of genetic modification used in agriculture. The first is through the process of **artificial selection**. Over time, farmers have picked the healthiest, most disease-resistant, best-producing strains of different crops to replant and grow, aiming for a more prosperous crop. This leads to higher crop yields, and in the case of fruits and vegetables, it can help lead to a more consistent-looking product, which is more appealing to a customer.

While artificial selection doesn't raise concerns of health risks, it does raise concerns over the growing vulnerability of crops to unforeseen problems. One example of this is the decline of the Gros Michel, a variety of banana. In the 1950s, the Gros Michel was the most popular banana breed available. However, since the Gros Michel banana didn't have seeds, the main way to make more banana trees was to take pieces of other trees and grow them into full trees. Soon, almost all banana plants were either clones or close cousins to each other. When a disease started to infect banana plants, there was nothing farmers could do but switch to a new kind of banana. The Cavendish has been the top banana ever since. However, banana growers continue to use the same methods as before, with a similar outcome. A new disease is affecting banana plantations all over the world, and the Cavendish may also be in danger.

The other type of genetic modification involves using science to examine the genes of a plant and make specific changes. By changing small parts of a plant's genes, they can be adapted in a lot of ways. They can be made more resistant to diseases. They can be made more tolerant to different growing conditions. Crops can also be modified so that chemicals used to kill or repel pests and weeds don't harm the crop. Genetic modification can even make crops poisonous to pests but harmless to humans. Lots of scientific research is still being conducted to find new ways to enhance crops to prepare for climate change.

Advancements for Developing Nations

Developing nations are very vulnerable to climate change. The Paris Agreement focuses a great deal on making sure technology and information are used to help poorer countries. The different tools and adaptations created for climate change can help these countries. Alternative energy sources can help developing nations and their economies. Economic growth enables a country to become more stable. It also enables them to participate more in international trade. Trade can lead to more advancements that help the developing world.

Advancements in agriculture can help prevent problems from scarcity or shortages after a disaster. If food supplies become more stable, they will allow for more people to work on other beneficial tasks. With food and water stability also comes better health.

Access to technology is also important to helping people with regard to climate change. The Paris Agreement encourages the sharing of technology and information. Technology can help to educate people, improving the lives of future generations. It can also be a tool for helping a developing nation take part in the international community more. As time has progressed, more countries are teaming up with developing nations. This helps the developing nations grow and also helps them prepare for the future.

4

Barriers to Cooperation

Even if many people think something is a good idea, that doesn't mean it will be easy. The world is a complicated place, with lots of perspectives and viewpoints on how best to do things. Protecting the planet is no exception. The makers of the Kyoto Protocol and Paris Agreement had several challenges to face in creating agreements that multiple nations could accept. Even after the Kyoto Protocol was created, it had some major obstacles before it could be passed.

Challenges with Economy

One of the primary challenges in passing treaties like the Kyoto Protocol involved concerns over its impact on the economies of participating countries. Fossil fuels were many nations' main resource for energy. While alternative energy sources existed, there wasn't enough cheap energy available. Forcing countries

Opposite: New York City is one of many cities that have thousands of people, each with different opinions, living there.

to suddenly shift from a cheap and powerful energy source to an expensive and weaker one could cause lots of problems. This is why the Kyoto Protocol was designed to give countries a few years to slowly change over time. The reasoning was that a slow conversion from fossil-fuel power to alternative power sources would have less of an impact on industry and the economy.

Even with a few years to reduce greenhouse gas emissions once the protocol went into effect in 2005, critics raised concerns over the speed at which countries were expected to reduce their emissions. They claimed that alternative energies were not powerful enough and too expensive. They also raised concerns over the lack of available replacements for cars and other vehicles that relied on fossil fuels. Although electric cars existed, they were not widely available or as affordable as fossil fuel–dependent cars. A lack of public transportation in countries like the United States, where most people have at least a fifteen-minute drive to work, could cause huge problems for their economy.

Another challenge faced by the Kyoto Protocol was the role of developing countries. Richer countries had higher goals for reduction than less-wealthy countries. Poorer countries were less able to make big changes that might harm their developing economies. The Kyoto Protocol tried to account for this by making several poorer countries exempt from the protocol. However, some people still felt it was unfair for richer countries to do most of the work.

Problematic Exemptions

The ultimate goal of the Kyoto Protocol was to reduce greenhouse gas emissions for each country to 5 percent below 1990 levels from 2008 to 2012. It also was designed so that countries that had more greenhouse gas emissions would need to reduce their emissions more drastically than other nations. According to the Union of Concerned Scientists, the five countries that produce the most greenhouse gas through burning fossil fuels are China, the United States, India, Russia, and Japan. As of 2005, all but the United States had agreed to it and signed it. However, one of the biggest challenges the Kyoto Protocol faced was the fact that China and India were exempt, meaning they didn't have to reduce their emissions if they didn't want to. Given this exemption, the two countries did not fully participate in the protocol.

This posed a significant risk to the implementation of the protocol. In order for it to pass, the nations involved had to account for 55 percent of Earth's man-made greenhouse gas emissions. India and China had some of the largest emission rates in the world. Without them, the 55 percent perhaps could not be reached and the protocol would fail to take effect.

The United States Doesn't Commit

In the planning stages of the Kyoto Protocol, which took place between 1998 and 2001 in different countries around the world, the United States seemed like they would participate in the treaty when the time came to ratify it. After all, Al Gore, a major activist for **environmentalism** and an educator about climate change and its implications, was the American vice president at that time, and he had helped write some of the initial protocol in 1997. The United States also had been one of the countries to sign on to the initial agreement before it was finalized. Since the United States is one of the top five contributors to greenhouse gas emissions, it was hoped to become one of the bigger frontiers for fighting climate change. However, as the protocol was further developed and finalized, the United States changed its political leaders and failed to get the Senate to agree to its terms.

Former US vice president Al Gore addressed the problem of climate change and its consequences in *An Inconvenient Truth*.

By the time the protocol was finalized and ready to be ratified, the United States had elected a new president who had other ideas for the country and didn't sign on. This put the protocol in jeopardy. Luckily, Russia and Japan, two other large contributors to greenhouse gas emissions, signed the protocol, giving it just enough signatories to pass.

Canada Drops Out

Even though the Kyoto Protocol passed, there were some who believed that the goals it set wouldn't be reached. Once in effect, it was realized by some that the goal of reducing emissions to 5 percent less than they were in 1990 would be difficult to achieve. With only four years to do it, some nations were concerned that there would be side effects, even if the goal was met.

Canada had ratified the agreement in 2005. By the time of implementation in 2008, it had taken steps to embrace the treaty. However, a change in government leaders who did not seem to think much of the treaty, as well as the prior leaders failing to take quicker action to produce results, prompted the nation to reconsider its involvement in 2011. One day after member nations met to discuss extending and amending the protocol, Canada officially withdrew its involvement.

Canada's main reasons for leaving the protocol were that it had failed to meet its reduction goal in such a short timeframe, and without the participation of the United States or China, the protocol seemed unfair and unfeasible. Canada's environmental minister, Peter Kent, said that the penalties from not meeting their goal were too harsh. Kent also said that dropping from the protocol would save Canada around $14 billion in penalties. Instead, the country decided to join a nonbinding agreement called the Copenhagen Accord. It was a treaty that targeted lowering greenhouse gas emissions too, but with no heavy fees if the targets

fact!

An Inconvenient Truth is a 2006 documentary based on a similarly titled book and presentation by Al Gore. It examines the possible damage and long-term effects of ignoring climate change. The film proved controversial when people who disagreed with Al Gore's politics or methods spoke out against the film, causing many to view climate change as part of a liberal political agenda. Nevertheless, it had a great effect on many people around the world.

Barack Obama

Barack Obama was born in Honolulu, Hawaii, in 1961. After graduating high school, he moved to Los Angeles, California, where he attended college. Later, he transferred to Columbia University to study political science. In 1997, he was elected to the Illinois state senate, and in 2005 he became a US senator for Illinois.

The forty-fourth president of the United States, Obama held office from 2009 to 2017. When he was elected, the Kyoto Protocol was in its first term. The United States couldn't rejoin the protocol, but President Obama still tried to fight climate change. In 2009, he passed the American Recovery and Reinvestment Act (ARRA). The ARRA aimed to fix economic problems as well as invest in renewable energy sources. Under Obama's administration, solar and wind energy were encouraged through tax credits, and other efforts were made to invest in clean energy sources. He also launched the Advanced Research Projects Administration-Energy (ARPA-E). ARPA-E was tasked with funding research and development of new energy technology.

The Obama administration also worked to make homes more energy efficient. To do this, it set new standards for efficiency for home appliances. It also invested in technologies to make homes able to generate some of their own energy through solar power. The Environmental Protection Agency (EPA) also mandated that major emitters of greenhouse gases had to report their emissions data to the EPA.

In 2010, on the fortieth anniversary of the first celebration of Earth Day, President Obama made a speech on the importance of protecting Earth and its climate. In it, he said, "Since taking office, my administration has been a partner in the fight for a healthier environment. Through the Recovery Act, we've invested in clean energy and clean water infrastructure across the country. We're taking the necessary steps to keep our children safe, and to hold polluters accountable. We've rejected the notion that we have to choose between creating jobs and a healthy environment."

Peter Kent, then Canada's environmental minister, on the day in 2011 when he announced Canada would leave the Kyoto Protocol

weren't met. Canada's goal for reducing greenhouse gas emissions in 2011 became to cut emissions by 17 percent of 2005 emissions. This was much less than reducing to levels below 1990 emissions.

With the loss of Canada's commitment to the Kyoto Protocol, other nations began to see that the challenges the protocol faced might be too much to tackle in one four-year term. In 2012, the Kyoto Protocol was extended to 2020, but many of the previous parties who signed on to the Kyoto Protocol's first term did not commit to the second. Instead, many nations chose to work toward a new agreement that would be more comprehensive.

Paris Agreement Problems

Started in 2015, the Paris Agreement seemed like it would fix a lot of problems the Kyoto Protocol had faced. For one, it was broader, had a goal of reducing the rise in global temperature, and gave specific greenhouse gas reduction goals for each nation. Canada was less likely to drop out because the United States, China, Japan, and India were all taking part in it. Many of the nations that did not commit to the second period of the Kyoto Protocol were also participating. The agreement was also regarded as a more complete international environmental agreement than the Kyoto Protocol. However, it had its own obstacles.

The United Nations Environmental Programme (UNEP) made one of the first criticisms against the Paris Agreement. By comparing scientific data with the goals listed in the Paris Agreement, the UNEP claimed that the Paris Agreement wouldn't succeed at slowing the rise in global temperature. Even if all of the Paris Agreement's goals for greenhouse gas reduction were met, the UNEP believed that the global temperature would rise a full degree above what the Paris Agreement hoped for. This is a big problem because even one-tenth of a degree over what the treaty was aiming for could be disastrous for Earth's environment. Also, the more damage done to the climate, the harder it would be to fix, as the effects of climate change would cause natural resource shortages.

Critics of the Paris Agreement also pointed out the fact that although it was an international treaty, it wasn't as binding as it could be. Many of the goals for individual nations were simple promises with no form of hard commitment. Any nation participating in the agreement may fail to meet its goals with little or no consequences from the international community. Normally, if a country did something that went against the rules set by the

United Nations, the other countries reacted using official policies that affected things like trade or diplomatic relations. However, since the Paris Agreement wasn't as binding as it could be, there would be no recourse for failure to deliver on promises made by a specific nation.

Another challenge faced by the Paris Agreement was the fact that fighting climate change takes time, and world leaders change over time. If a new world leader was elected who didn't value fighting climate change, it was feared they could stop working toward the Paris Agreement. It can take years for progress to be made toward fighting climate change. If a world leader decided not to participate or even worked to undo the progress of the Paris Agreement, it could cause a lot of damage to the climate. This is a significant risk because any time a new world leader is elected, they might influence or even eliminate the work toward fulfilling the Paris Agreement's goals. The United States experienced a version of this problem in 2017.

In June of that year, the world became aware of the very real consequences that a change of leadership could cause for an accord such as the Paris Agreement. On June 1, 2017, US president Donald Trump said that the United States would withdraw from the Paris Agreement. This change wouldn't be complete until 2020, when nations in the Paris Agreement are allowed to officially leave. However, its effects caused reactions around the world and within the United States.

Many other world leaders remained committed to fighting climate change; however, they expressed shock and concern over the US president's announcement. Without US involvement, they feared other countries might also withdraw from the agreement. German chancellor Angela Merkel said, "The decision for the United States to pull out of the Paris Agreement is utterly regrettable, and that is me using very restrained language."

United States president Donald Trump announces the United States' withdrawal from the Paris Agreement.

French president Emmanuel Macron also spoke on the United States' withdrawal: "I wish to tell the United States, France believes in you. The world believes in you. I know you are a great nation. I know our common history. To all scientists, engineers, entrepreneurs, and responsible citizens who were disappointed by the decision of the president of the United States, I want to say you will find in France a second homeland. I call on them: 'Come here, and work with us.'"

Climate Change Deniers in Positions of Power

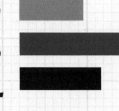

Some people don't believe in climate change. They don't understand the science or they disregard it. A few have been convinced by industry leaders that it's either not real or not a problem. Although the effects of climate change are becoming harder to ignore, current and future climate action is hampered by climate change denial. This is especially true when climate change deniers are put in positions of power.

According to Skeptical Science, a website dedicated to dispelling myths used to criticize or deny the issue of climate change, depending on the statistical measurement used, at least 90 percent of scientists agree that climate change is an issue and is caused largely by human activity. It is a significant problem, therefore, when an individual who doesn't think climate change exists rises to a position of power where he or she has the ability to stop actions meant to fight climate change or simply cause more of the public opinion to sway on the issue of climate change.

One such example is Scott Pruitt. In 2016, President Donald Trump nominated him to the position of administrator of the EPA. The EPA is tasked with enforcing the legislation the United States has passed to protect its air, water, and

EPA administrator Scott Pruitt addresses a White House press briefing in June 2017.

natural landscapes, such as the Clean Air Act and the Clean Water Act.

Pruitt denies the scientific consensus on the existence of climate change and has publicly stated that he doesn't believe human activity and the burning of fossil fuels are the primary cause. For years prior to his appointment as head of the EPA, Pruitt worked to strike down regulations on industry aiming to protect the environment and has had ties with lobbyists and heads of industry deeply invested in fossil fuels. It is uncertain what positive effect Pruitt will have on the EPA, but he may lead ultimately to the organization's demise.

Within the United States itself, several state leaders took it upon themselves to rise to the challenge and commit to the global reductions presented in the Paris Agreement. States such as California, New York, and Hawaii joined the United States Climate Alliance, which would help them meet greenhouse gas emission goals laid out by the treaty. Officials in states such as Montana, Colorado, and Illinois agreed to follow the Paris Agreement but did not join the US Climate Alliance.

Many industrial leaders were also disappointed in the president's decision. Executives from Google, Microsoft, Apple, and Facebook all expressed the need for the United States to be a leader in climate-change work. Tesla CEO Elon Musk also resigned from his position on two of the president's advisory councils after the announcement was made to leave the Paris Agreement.

fact! Economic Impact of Climate Change

One major area of research in wind energy is the possibility of offshore wind generators. Crews could live and work on offshore habitats around wind generators, similar to offshore oil platforms today.

One of the biggest challenges facing both the Kyoto Protocol and the Paris Agreement is the effect of climate change on economies worldwide. On one hand, climate change can cause damage to many natural resources around the globe. This could lead to some products becoming much harder and more expensive to create. On the other hand, drastic actions to eliminate fossil fuels could also cause problems. Industries that rely on fossil fuels would need to seek ways to reduce emissions or new fuels entirely, and both tasks are expensive. Workers in fossil fuel industries or whose jobs depend on fossil fuels could also suffer unemployment. Most people also can't afford to eliminate their current cars and trucks for electronic vehicles. Also, the trucking industry doesn't currently have clear options for reducing their emissions either. It is clear that fighting climate change and preserving economies are both important goals.

To overcome these obstacles, the Paris Agreement incorporates working with the Green Climate Fund (GCF). The GCF is tasked by the United Nations with helping ease the economic strain of developing and incorporating changes.

Another way this challenge is being worked on is by framing alternative energies as an opportunity for economic growth. Groups like the Solar Energy Industry Association (SEIA) are trying to show that opportunity. According to the SEIA website: "The solar industry is one of the fastest-growing industries in the nation and offers tremendous opportunities for workers from all backgrounds." The SEIA holds workshops to train people in areas related to the solar power industry.

Similarly, the American Wind Energy Association trains more people to work with sources of wind energy every year. With other sources of energy growing quickly in the United States and around the world, both jobs and energy sources may shift and change to cleaner energy sources.

5

The Legacy of International Environmental Protection

I t's true that decades of industrial activity have damaged our world. However, people have proven time and time again that it's possible to change the world if we work together. Working toward a goal of preserving the ozone layer in the 1980s and 1990s was one example. Yet there is still a lot of work to be done for the other problems that humans have caused for the environment. International agreements like the Kyoto Protocol and the Paris Agreement are steps in the right direction.

A Need for More

In order to fight climate change, the world will likely need more agreements. Perhaps these will be many smaller agreements introduced over time, or a few larger accords meant to bring drastic change. In the meantime, the Paris Agreement and Kyoto Protocol are the two main accords we have. Those agreements

Opposite: If people work together, they can ensure the world and its beautiful places are preserved and protected for years to come.

need to continue to be enforced and modified to keep up with changes in the world.

Currently, the Kyoto Protocol is in its second term, set to end in 2020. Since it has been overshadowed in some ways by the newer Paris Agreement, it might eventually be phased out in favor of the new treaty. The Paris Agreement, meanwhile, might also be modified to be more comprehensive. For example, it might start to cover some of the things that the Kyoto Protocol once oversaw, making the end of the protocol more likely. As new technologies, policies, and world events shape the future, new agreements might come about, or current ones could change further.

As we have seen before, if a new need arises, new agreements can be made. If a species important to the international community is endangered, for example, a new agreement might be made to protect that species. If a new resource or technology is shown to be helpful in fighting climate change, new policies might encourage further developments. Much like Earth's ecosystem, humanity's role in the future of preserving the planet will be in a cycle of cause and effect.

A Cycle to Recovery

In the meantime, the effects of climate change will continue to occur, likely getting a bit worse before they start to get better. As carbon dioxide is released into the atmosphere through the burning of fossil fuels, it will trap heat in the atmosphere. All matter expands when heated, including water, and as water is both plentiful and has a significant rate of expansion due to heat, a rise in global average temperature will cause the water in Earth's oceans to expand. In fact, climate scientists have already measured a rise in water levels and have concluded that the rate at which it is rising is only getting faster.

Countries and cities that have a lot of coastline could be greatly affected by rising water levels. Venice, Italy, for example, is seeing more severe seasonal and tidal flooding, prompting a need for new methods of holding back tidal waters. If rising waters become more of a widespread issue, international agreements might also be called for.

fact!

Scientists estimate that sea levels could rise as much as 5 feet (1.5 meters) by the end of the year 2100.

As carbon dioxide mixes with ocean water, it creates small amounts of carbonic acid. This changes the chemical composition of the water enough to pose a risk to many types of oceanic microbiology as well as coral reefs, which are dying off and becoming "bleached" as their skeletons are left behind. This sudden change in the oceanic ecosystem could cause great damage to countries that rely on ocean fishing for food or business.

As the global average temperature rises, global weather patterns will become more severe, resulting in harsher storms and droughts. Rainfall cycles will become more hostile to different crops. Crops like cocoa beans and coffee beans will become harder to grow in higher temperatures, meaning products made from them will become scarce and more expensive. Scientists are working to find ways to adapt crops to future climate change, but crops are still at risk. As temperatures rise even further, plants that can't stand the heat will die off or only survive at higher altitudes where it is cooler, leaving fewer plants for herbivores and omnivores to eat. Further, as glaciers and sea ice shrink in the rising temperature, animals that rely on those ice formations will be at further risk.

People plant trees in an effort to help the environment.

As the environment changes, people will need to change as well. As the climate makes places harder for people to live, more places will become more populated. It's entirely possible that new nations might be created by changes in geography brought about by Earth's changing climate. The international community will need to adapt to the changes brought about by humanity's actions. New technology, new resources, and new policies will all play a part in how countries will band together to work toward the future.

Ways Forward

Protecting the planet will not be an easy task, even with countries working together. There will always be obstacles to overcome. There will always be people who stand in the way of fighting climate change, either to preserve their wealth and influence or simply because they don't believe climate change exists.

However, it's important to keep in mind that the majority of people agree climate change is a big issue and there should be efforts made to reduce greenhouse gas emissions. Peaceful solutions through diplomacy, education, and partnership have been and will continue to be made. In time, with enough work, Earth can be preserved.

Even after the Paris Agreement and other possible iterations of it come into effect, Earth's climate will not change immediately. It may take years, even decades, to undo the damage that has been done. At times, it might seem silly to work to fix a problem that people might not live to see solved. But nobody has ever solved every problem in a single lifetime. Humans working together can overcome all sorts of boundaries and achieve many goals.

fact!

The last century has been a mixed blessing for human civilization. During that time, we have developed amazing tools and technologies that have become more advanced and more powerful as they evolve, allowing us to tackle obstacles in seconds when at one time it would have taken days or weeks. However, the creation of these tools comes with a toll that humans must keep in mind in the future. Are we willing to suffer the cost of an increasingly hostile planet for these technologies? Are we willing to gamble on the creation of technology that will allow us to travel to another habitable planet before Earth, our only home, becomes too damaged to sustain human life, or any life, for that matter?

One of the most recyclable plastics is high-density polyethylene, or HDPE, the plastic used to make milk jugs and other containers. Because it's strong, nontoxic, and easily reused, HDPE can be used in everything from toys to tool handles.

A Blue Marble image taken by NASA in 2011. This photo shows Earth's eastern hemisphere.

The risks of underestimating the problem of a changing climate are too great to ignore. After all, this planet is the only one humans have for the foreseeable future.

The future may never be completely certain, but human beings have the incredible ability to observe, to measure, to learn and understand, to predict future events based on trends, and to pass on the lessons we have learned to future generations. The journey will be long and difficult, and will require facing obstacles in the form of technological limits and individuals or groups that fail to understand or acknowledge the problem of climate change, but the chance to make the world a better one is worth the effort. It is worth the time spent measuring and crafting legislation and communicating with one another because those things are what humans do best. We collaborate, we cooperate, we innovate, and we find ways to do the impossible.

Environmental Preservation Activities

There are many ways someone can help preserve the health of the planet, such as recycling and reducing the use of fossil fuels. However, to make a big difference, it is best to have a group of people taking action. After all, the more people who get involved with a cause, the more success the group tends to have. Here are some activities small groups can do to help make a positive impact:

1) Planting bee-friendly herbs and flowers in gardens and window boxes will help pollinators survive and thrive in difficult temperatures.

2) By combining clay, wildflower seeds, and a bit of powdered plant food into spheres about the size of a Ping-Pong ball, a small group of workers can make "seed bombs." These can be tossed onto dirt lots, ditches, and other natural areas to create a "starter kit" for the seeds' growth.

3) Many towns and cities have community gardens that need volunteers to help care for them. A quick search around the neighborhood might reveal great places to get involved. If there isn't one in the area, another activity might be to find a way to start one.

4) Organizing a plant sale, bake sale, or other fundraising activity on Arbor Day or Earth Day is a great way to raise funds that can be donated to local or nonprofit organizations that can use the funds to make a positive impact on the environment.

Glossary

agriculture The science and practices of farming.

alternative energy Forms of energy, such as electricity, that are generated by sources other than the burning of fossil fuels.

apiary A place where bees and beehives are kept to produce honey, beeswax, and other related products.

artificial selection The process of identifying desirable traits in crops and growing them to make those traits more common.

chlorofluorocarbons A type of chemical that contains compounds with carbon, chlorine, or fluorine.

combustible fuels Fuels that catch fire or burn easily, like coal and petroleum.

deforestation The practice of removing areas of forest or rain forest to make space for housing or development and to gather lumber.

ecosystem A community of animals, plants, and other species that exist together in one area and depend on each other.

environmentalism The idea that the natural environment should be protected in some way.

fossil fuel Fuel derived from ancient organisms. Typically, it is burned to release energy. This includes petroleum and coal.

genetically modified organisms Organisms changed by scientifically modifying the genes of a plant or animal to give it traits beneficial to the process of its cultivation.

greenhouse effect The process by which gases like carbon dioxide traps more heat in Earth's atmosphere, similar to how the physical walls of a greenhouse trap heat inside.

greenhouse gas Gases such as carbon dioxide and methane that contribute to the "greenhouse effect" by trapping heat in Earth's atmosphere.

Holy See The jurisdiction of the Catholic Church in Rome, Italy.

ozone-depleting chemicals A classification of chemicals known to contribute to the depletion of the ozone laycr by binding with the ozone atoms, thereby changing their properties.

ozone layer A layer of Earth's atmosphere that absorbs and dissipates ultraviolet radiation that comes from the sun.

photovoltaic panels Devices used to convert light into electricity.

preservation The idea that the environment is best protected by leaving as much of it untouched or affected by human developments as possible.

signatory Someone who signs a document along with other people.

space race A period from the 1950s to 1970s characterized by the competition between the United States and the Soviet Union to land on the moon.

ultraviolet ray A type of electromagnetic radiation that is produced by the sun. In large quantities it can cause harm to humans, such as cancers.

United Nations An international organization of countries from around the world intended to help different countries cooperate in different international efforts.

Further Information

Books

Kolbert, Elizabeth. *The Sixth Extinction: An Unnatural History*. New York: Henry Holt and Co., 2014.

Marshall, George. *Don't Even Think About It: Why Our Brains Are Wired to Ignore Climate Change*. New York: Bloomsbury Publishing, 2014.

McMichael, Anthony. *Climate Change and the Health of Nations: Famines, Fevers, and the Fate of Populations*. New York: Oxford University Press, 2017.

Orsekes, Naomi, and Erik M Conway. *Merchants of Doubt: How a Handful of Scientists Obscured the Truth on Issues from Tobacco Smoke to Global Warming*. New York: Bloomsbury Publishing, 2010.

Romm, Joseph. *Climate Change: What Everyone Needs to Know*. Oxford, UK: Oxford University Press, 2015.

Websites

Climate Change: How Do We Know?

https://climate.nasa.gov/evidence

This is a collection of officially documented evidence gathered by the National Aeronautics and Space Administration (NASA) of the changes in Earth's climate.

The Environmental Protection Agency

https://www.epa.gov

This is the official website of the EPA.

The Intergovernmental Panel on Climate Change

http://www.ipcc.ch

The official website for the IPCC stores the reports of scientific findings on climate change that the United Nations has used to determine international environmental policies.

The Kyoto Protocol

https://www.britannica.com/event/Kyoto-Protocol

This article discusses more about the history of the Kyoto Protocol.

Organizations

International Union for Conservation of Nature

https://www.iucn.org

The IUCN works internationally to advocate for policies that promote sustainable industrial and agricultural practices and for the conservation of nature.

The National Park Service

https://www.nps.gov/index.htm

The National Park Service oversees more than four hundred national parks in the United States, as well as many of the nation's national monuments. They also take part in services that educate people about nature and the environment.

The Sierra Club

http://www.sierraclub.org

The Sierra Club is an environmental organization founded in the late 1800s. It is now one of the largest organizations advocating for conservation, preservation, and ethical environmental policies and practices.

United Nations

http://www.un.org/en/index.html

This is the main unifying body of countries around the world. They have banded together to make joint decisions on important aspects such as human rights, human safety, and climate change.

Bibliography

American Wind Energy Association. http://www.awea.org.

"Ban Ki-moon Secretary-General." United Nations.
https://www.un.org/sg/en/formersg/ban.shtml.

"Barack Obama." Biography.com. June 1, 2017. https://
www.biography.com/people/barack-obama-12782369.

"A Brief Timeline of the History of Recycling." Busch
Systems Resource Center, April 14, 2016. https://
www.buschsystems.com/resource-center/page/a-
brief-timeline-of-the-history-of-recycling.

"Canada Pulls Out of Kyoto Protocol."
Guardian, December 12, 2011. https://
www.theguardian.com/environment/2011/
dec/13/canada-pulls-out-kyoto-protocol.

"Christiana Figueres' Biography." GLOBE International.
http://globelegislators.org/events/2013/1gcls-
home/66-events/climate-legislation-
summit/142-christiana-figueres-biography.

"Climate Science Glossary." Skeptical Science.
https://www.skepticalscience.com.

"Dr. Rajendra Kumar Pachauri, Nobel Peace Prize Winner 2007." *Majalla,* December 27, 2009. http://eng.majalla.com/2009/12/article5512570/dr-rajendra-kumar-pachauri-nobel-peace-prize-winner-2007.

"Environmental History Timeline." Environmentalhistory.org. Accessed April 2017. http://environmentalhistory.org.

Gore, Al. *An Inconvenient Truth.* London: Bloomsbury Publishing, 2006.

Grossman, Jonathan. "History – The Coal Strike of 1902; Turning Point in U.S. Policy." US Department of Labor. https://www.dol.gov/oasam/programs/history/coalstrike.htm.

Hartman, Holly. "Milestones in Environmental Protection." Infoplease. https://www.infoplease.com/spot/milestones-environmental-protection.

"Industrial Revolution." History.com. 2009. http://www.history.com/topics/industrial-revolution.

Intergovernmental Panel on Climate Change. http://www.ipcc.ch.

Lear, Linda. "Rachel Carson's Biography." http://www.rachelcarson.org/Bio.aspx.

Mann, Michael E., and Tom Toles. *The Madhouse Effect: How Climate Change Denial Is Threatening Our Planet, Destroying Our Politics, and Driving Us Crazy.* New York: Columbia University Press, 2016.

Nuclear Energy Institute. https://www.nei.org.

"Official ARPA-E Homepage." ARPA-E. June 14, 2017. https://arpa-e.energy.gov.

"Paris Agreement: Status of Ratification." United Nations Framework Convention on Climate Change. April 25, 2017. http://unfccc.int/2860.php.

Recycle Across America, Standardized Recycling Labels. http://www.recycleacrossamerica.org.

Sachs, Jeffrey D. *The Age of Sustainable Development.* New York: Columbia University Press, 2015.

Sanger, David E. "Bush Will Continue to Oppose Kyoto Pact on Global Warming." *New York Times*, June 11, 2001. http://www.nytimes.com/2001/06/12/world/bush-will-continue-to-oppose-kyoto-pact-on-global-warming.html.

Shear, Michael D. "Trump Will Withdraw U.S. from Paris Climate Agreement." *New York Times*, June 01, 2017. https://www.nytimes.com/2017/06/01/climate/trump-paris-climate-agreement.html?_r=0.

"Solar Energy Industries Association." Solar
   Energy Industries Association. April 27,
   2017. http://www.seia.org.

Suzuki, David T., and Ian Hanington. *Just Cool It!: The Climate
   Crisis and What We Can Do: A Post-Paris Agreement Game
   Plan*. Vancouver, Canada: Greystone Books, 2017.

Trueman, C. N. "Diseases in Industrial Cities in the
   Industrial Revolution." History Learning Site.
   http://www.historylearningsite.co.uk/britain-
   1700-to-1900/industrial-revolution/diseases-in-
   industrial-cities-in-the-industrial-revolution.

Index

sea levels, 39, 43, 92–93

seed bombs, 97

signatory, 31, 78

solar power, 53, 58–59,
    60, 61, 64, 80–81, 89

space race, 5–6

steam engine, 13

storms, 44, 65, 93

strike, 16

Syria, 35, 38

Technology Mechanism,
    44–46

Trump, Donald, 38,
    55, 84, **85**, 86

Tyndall, John, 14

ultraviolet ray, 21

Union of Concerned
    Scientists, 77

United Nations, 9, 17, 25,
    27, 29–30, 35–37, 42,
    46–47, 53–55, 83–84, 89

United Nations
    Environmental
    Programme (UNEP), 83

United Nations Framework
    Convention on Climate
    Change (UNFCCC), 27,
    29, 33, 35, 38, 44-48, 55

United States, 11, 13–14, **15**,
    17–19, 25, 30–31, 35, 38,
    45, 54–56, 76–80, 83–89

US Climate Alliance, 88

US Forest Service, 18

Warsaw International
    Mechanism, 44, 46

water filters, 65–66

wind power, 16, **52**, 53,
    58–59, 61, 80, 88–89

World Meteorological
    Association, 25

World Resources Institute, 50

Yosemite National
    Park, 18 19

About the Author

Jordan Johnson is an avid reader and all-around science enthusiast from Wisconsin. He studied earth science, geography, and environmental issues during his time at the University of Wisconsin–River Falls. He has also worked with small businesses to reduce their greenhouse gas emissions. Together with his wife, he makes handmade soap, plays computer games, and recycles whenever possible.